The Blizzard Challenge

BEAR GRYLLS ADVENTURES

The **BEAR GRYLLS ADVENTURES** series

The Blizzard Challenge

The Desert Challenge

The Jungle Challenge

The Sea Challenge

The River Challenge

The Earthquake Challenge

The Volcano Challenge

The Safari Challenge

The Cave Challenge

The Mountain Challenge

The Arctic Challenge

The Sailing Challenge

The **Blizzard** Challenge

Bear Grylls

Illustrated by Emma McCann

Bear
Grylls

First American Edition 2017
Kane Miller, A Division of EDC Publishing

First published in Great Britain in 2017 by Bear Grylls, an imprint
of Bonnier Zaffre, a Bonnier Publishing Company
Text and illustrations copyright © Bear Grylls Ventures, 2017
Illustrations by Emma McCann

For information contact:
Kane Miller, A Division of EDC Publishing
5402 S 122nd E Ave
Tulsa, OK 74146
www.kanemiller.com
www.myubam.com

Library of Congress Control Number: 2017945579

Printed and bound in the United States of America
7 8 9 10 11 12 13 14 15

ISBN: 978-1-68464-125-3

*To the young adventurer
reading this book for the first time.
May your eyes always be wide-open
to adventure, and your heart full
of courage and determination to
see your dreams through.*

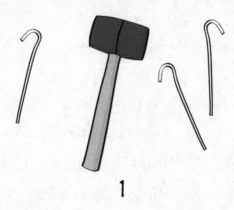

1

KILLER BACKPACK, HORRIBLE TENT

Olly decided he wasn't going to enjoy camp when his backpack tried to kill him.

He had gotten a ride with his friend Jack, who'd been before. Jack's dad pulled into the parking lot and Jack leaped out to go and report to one of the leaders. Olly got out more slowly while Jack's dad popped the truck open. Olly grabbed his backpack, and pulled.

It didn't budge, but Olly almost fell over.

"It's heavy," he protested.

"Well, there is a lot in it," Jack's dad replied. He lifted it out. "I couldn't believe everything they told Jack to bring. Sleeping bag, climbing boots, running shoes, towels, umpteen changes of clothes ... didn't you notice when you packed?"

"My dad did it," Olly said.

"Oh, right." Jack's dad helped Olly get the backpack onto his back. Olly almost fell over again. "It's a shame both your parents had to work this weekend. They do work hard, don't they?"

"I suppose," Olly muttered. They had said the camp was a treat to make up for it. He would have rather just stayed at home alone, but apparently he wasn't old enough yet. Home had everything he needed. Food, television and no one else around.

Jack came running back.

"We have to check in together. Then we'll find out who we're in a tent with." His big smile said he was so looking forward to this.

"Well, I'll see you in a couple of days, then." Jack got a hug from his dad. Olly got a friendly pat on the shoulder. "Enjoy yourselves!"

Olly watched the car drive off. Then he turned and glumly followed Jack.

The leader was a smiling woman with a clipboard. She took their names, and then called another boy over.

"This is Omar," she said. "We're

putting everyone into threes, and you're sharing a tent together."

"Hi, Omar," Jack said happily. "Pleased to meet you. I'm Jack and this is my friend Olly."

"Sure," Omar said. He smiled back, but he was already turning away like he was impatient to get on. "I found where

we get the tents from," he called over his shoulder. "Let's go!"

"Wow, he's keen, isn't he?" Jack commented as they set off after him.

So, that's two of them, Olly thought to himself.

They were given their tent and equipment in a huge bag that was so heavy all three had to carry it between them to a spot at the campsite.

Then they had to put it up.

It wasn't a modern pop-up tent, where you threw it onto the ground and it shot up like magic. Nothing so easy.

"Okay," Omar said. "I've done this before. We have to fit these together so they stand up, then we hang the canvas on the frame. So we just have to find the parts that go together."

They started to rummage through the pile of poles. Olly soon found a couple that seemed to fit, and it looked like Omar had a couple that would screw into the ones he had. Olly put his poles down so that Omar could use them when he was ready, and looked through the pile to see which other ones went together.

"Come on!" Omar said impatiently after a moment.

Olly looked up. "What?"

"Pass them over!" Omar pointed at the poles Olly had put down. "I've got a whole bunch that fit here – I just need those ones."

"I was *about* to pass them to you," Olly said. Omar got up to fetch them, rolling his eyes and muttering under his breath.

After that they had to put the frame

over the groundsheet,
then drag the canvas over
the whole thing and tie it on.
Finally, they had to hammer
pegs into the ground and attach
guy ropes to them, to make
sure the tent didn't blow away in
the wind.

"Okay," Omar said, "I know how to
do the ropes."

Jack and Olly looked at each other.

"You hammer in the pegs, then attach
the ropes and tighten them, don't you?"
Jack asked.

Omar shook his head.

"Nope. It's better than that.
You make the ropes as tight as
possible *while* you hammer the
peg in. That way the peg makes

them even tighter. So all three of us will have to do each rope – two of us pull and one of us hammers."

So Olly put the first peg through a loop at the end of the first guy rope, while Jack and Omar pulled. Olly gave the peg a thwack with a rubber mallet.

The mallet bounced back and almost hit him in the eye. The peg didn't budge.

"Whoa!" he shouted.

"You okay?" Jack asked.

Olly tried again, but still the peg wouldn't go in.

"The ground's too hard!" he moaned.

"I'll do it." Omar grabbed the mallet from Olly before he could say anything. Olly took Omar's place and pulled on the rope with Jack. Omar shifted the peg just a little to the left and hammered it in, no problem. Olly turned an embarrassed red.

"You were over a stone," Omar said scornfully. "Let's get the others done. Only five more to go …"

Omar kept the mallet to do the rest.

When all the tents were up, one of the leaders walked into the middle of the campsite and blew a whistle.

"Okay, everyone, now that we're all here, let's head to the meeting place."

"Time to move!" Omar exclaimed. He hurried straight off, gesturing at the other two to follow. Jack started to move, then realized Olly was lagging behind.

"Coming?" he asked. He did a little dance to show he really wanted to go.

"Yeah," Olly muttered. "Coming."

He followed them with his hands in his pockets, dragging his feet slowly.

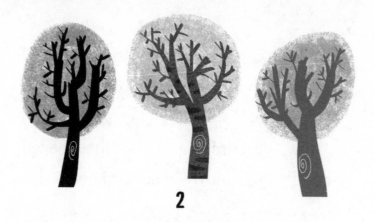

2

DENS AND DUCKING OUT

In a sandy clearing in the middle of the woods a man was shouting instructions.

"We're going to finish today with a barbecue, but first, this afternoon's challenge is to build a den with your tentmates. You have three hours. Use whatever you find in the woods, bring it back here and we'll build our dens together." He paused. "First team to complete their den gets a prize. And you'll also get points for style, original thinking, how weatherproof it is … you get the idea!"

Olly certainly got the idea, even though he couldn't believe his ears. He nudged Jack.

"We're going to spend the afternoon making dens?" he asked. Just in case he had misheard.

"Yup," Jack replied.

"Why are we making dens when we've got tents?"

"Because it's fun," Jack said.

Olly rolled his eyes. This whole camp thing was just one pointless activity after another.

Jack, Olly and Omar set off into the woods and before long they came to a clearing where there were piles of logs,

branches and sticks just perfect for den making. A lot of the other kids had had the same idea. There was plenty of laughing and friendly bickering as they all tried to be the first ones to get the really good pieces of wood.

Olly was half-heartedly tugging at

a branch when an ear-splitting shriek made him jump so fast he thought he pulled a muscle. A girl on the other side of the log pile was staring at something in front of her.

"Could you scream a bit louder?" he asked sarcastically.

She scowled and pointed.

"There's a massive spider!"

Olly peered over. The spider was about an inch across, which he didn't think was massive at all.

"I just have a problem with creepy-crawlies," she added apologetically.

She looked miserable and Olly was sorry for being sarcastic. But he didn't get a chance to say anything else because just then –

"Olly! Stop talking and get over here!" Omar shouted impatiently.

It took Olly less than twenty seconds to get to where Jack and Omar were, but Omar glared at him like he had held them up for hours.

He showed Olly the pieces of wood he and Jack had pulled together.

"These are the right length and strength," he said. "We'll use these for the basic structure."

Olly groaned to himself. It would be like putting the tent up all over again. But harder because these branches weren't designed to go together.

"And then we can find smaller ones with lots of leaves," Jack agreed, "and use them to make a roof and walls to keep the rain and wind out ..."

"Yeah, but first we need to get these back to the meeting place," said Omar. "First team gets a prize, remember? Let's go!"

They each had two large branches to carry. Jack wrapped his arms around both and carried them across his chest. Omar stuck one over each shoulder and kept them steady with his hands. They both set off.

Olly tried it Jack's way first, but the wood felt too heavy. And the ends kept getting in the way. So he tried it Omar's way. His shoulders weren't used to that kind of weight, and the wood kept rolling off.

Eventually he tried to drag his pieces on the ground. That stopped his shoulders aching, but it actually turned out to be hardest of all. The ends kept getting tangled in the undergrowth and the wood was yanked out of his hands.

"Come on, Olly!" Omar called from up ahead. "We'll run out of time!"

So stop shouting and start building, Olly thought with gritted teeth. Eventually Olly reluctantly decided that Jack's way was best, even though it made his arms ache. He caught up with the other two at the meeting place and dropped the logs.

"Okay, now we need the small stuff," Omar said, hurrying off again. "Another couple of hours and we'll be done!"

As Jack and Omar headed back into the woods, Olly's heart sank. A couple more hours of making this silly den. What was the point?

He stopped suddenly as the thought struck him.

That's right. What was the point?

Answer: there wasn't one.

Omar and Jack could obviously do it without him. So why didn't he just leave them to it?

And so Olly went slower and slower,

and the others got farther
and farther ahead of him.
Then he swung off to the
right and started to pick up
his pace. The trees grew closer
together. Where there weren't
trees, there was tall bracken.

Soon he couldn't see anyone
else, just hear voices. A couple
of times he heard a scream, so he
guessed the girl from the woodpile
had seen another spider.

Score! Olly thought. Now he
could spend the afternoon in
the tent listening to music.
It wouldn't be as good as
being at home watching
TV, but it was better than *this*.

"Are you lost?" said a girl's voice

right behind him. "You're on your own."

Olly almost jumped out of his skin. He hadn't heard her come up.

"Uh … I'm just going this way," he said, pointing through the woods. It was true. He was going to where the tents were.

"You don't look like you're enjoying camp," she said. It was like she could read his mind, and Olly couldn't think of a good answer. "I think you need this."

She held something out and Olly took it. It was a compass. There was nothing special about it. It had a transparent

21

plastic dial, with a needle that always swung slowly to point north. Why did he need a compass? He could find his way on his own.

But when he looked up the girl was already walking off. So he slipped the compass into his pocket anyway and continued to head back to the tent.

3

FIFTH DIRECTION

"This is awful," Olly muttered.

He lay on top of his sleeping bag and stared at the canvas ceiling of the tent.

He was finally doing what he wanted. But when he tried to focus on his book, the words just seemed to swim around in front of his eyes. He couldn't make himself care about the story. And the music on his iPod sounded dull and flat.

He felt guilty, and even more bored than before.

Olly sighed. Okay, this had been a bad idea. If he had to be bored then he might as well do it with the others. Even Omar.

He got up, and headed back to the woods.

It took Olly a while to find Jack and Omar among all the other kids racing around still gathering den material. Eventually he saw Jack in the distance through the trees, carrying a heap of fern leaves. It looked like he could use a hand. Olly set off after him.

Omar and Jack were building their den at the edge of the meeting place. As Olly made his way through the trees he got quite close to them without their realizing. Hearing their voices made him smile. He had sort of missed them. Jack was his friend and Omar was ... okay,

Omar wasn't his friend. Not exactly. But he wasn't nasty. Just a bit impatient.

Then he heard what the boys were saying. "I don't know why you bother with that loser Olly," Omar said to Jack. "Hey, Olly's not –" Jack began.

"Well, he's not here, is he?" Omar snapped. "We can do it without him. Here, help me tie this."

Olly stood where he was, stunned.

So, he thought, *now I know what Omar thinks of me.*

And what was he supposed to do now?

Pretend he hadn't heard? He turned around and went back to the tent.

Olly lay on his sleeping bag. Again. This time he was both bored *and* upset. And now that he came to think about it, he was also hungry. It was time for the barbecue, so everyone would be snacking on delicious burgers and sausages.

But Olly didn't want to face Omar.

So he just lay there alone for what felt like forever.

* * *

Eventually it started to get dark, and Olly heard voices getting nearer. The barbecue was over and it was time for bed. Jack and Omar pushed their way through the tent flap. Omar's lip curled slightly when he saw Olly, like he thought Olly smelled. Jack just looked sad.

27

"We built a really good den," Jack said after a moment. "You'd have liked it."

"Did you win the prize?" Olly asked.

"No," Omar told him abruptly. "Because there were only *two* of us. We needed three to get everything done in time."

After that, no one said anything much. The boys got ready for bed and slid into their sleeping bags. Outside, the camp was going quiet. Soon, Olly could tell from the sound of Jack and Omar's breathing that they were asleep. He could still hear voices outside, from other tents, but one by one they went silent. He lay in his sleeping bag, feeling wide-awake.

He could still hear Omar's words in his head. Somehow Olly had to get through the rest of the camp knowing what Omar

really thought about him. And Jack was obviously disappointed with him too.

At least if he could sleep, Olly thought, it would be over quicker. He often fell asleep listening to music, so he felt in the dark for his iPod. The screen lit up, just in time for him to see the words CONNECT TO POWER SOURCE. Then it went blank.

Olly groaned and let his hand flop back with the dead iPod. Something hard and plastic knocked against his knuckles. What was that? He held it up in front of his face so that he could see it in the dim light. Oh, yeah. The compass.

Suddenly the compass dial lit up, as if a light had come on behind it. That was weird because there was nowhere for a battery to go. He could make out the needle, and the four illuminated markings for North, South, East and West. They were just bright enough for him to see without being able to read. He turned it idly in his hands, watching the needle stay on North.

But then the needle seemed to be turning on its own. Olly watched as it slowly spun through North, East, South,

West and
stopped on a fifth marking.

"Huh?!" Olly said out loud. He couldn't hide his surprise. How were there suddenly *five* directions?

Jack and Omar stirred, but didn't wake up.

Olly looked around suspiciously. Thinking. Looking for an explanation. Then he looked back at the compass. He couldn't see in the dim light what the fifth direction was called. But he could see that the needle was pointing out of the tent. Just as he looked over at the flap, a gust of cold wind blew through and he gasped. It was so cold, it was like someone had slid a knife made of ice under his skin. Absolutely freezing.

Olly clambered over to zip the flap completely closed. Suddenly bright sunlight shone into the tent. Olly blinked hard, paused, then slowly crawled out and stood up. He stared in astonishment at what he saw.

He should have been in the middle of the campsite, surrounded by tents. And it should have been nighttime.

In fact, it was daylight and he was standing on rocky ground covered with bright-white snow, surrounded by giant mountains.

"What ...?"

It was freezing, even though the sun was shining so brightly in the blue sky that Olly had to screw his eyes to slits. He wrapped his arms around himself. He could feel the cold eating into his bones.

"Hey!" A man's voice shouted in his ear. "Quick, or you'll freeze to death!"

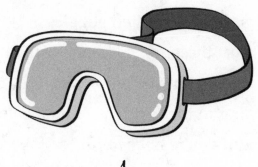

4

MANY WAYS TO DIE

Olly was now shivering so much he could barely look around.

"What's h-app-en-ed, wh-ere am I …?" he mumbled through chattering teeth. He was still wearing the shorts and T-shirt he had put on to go to bed. The tent and everything else he knew had vanished.

The man was rummaging through a bulky backpack, but despite the cold the first thing he handed Olly wasn't clothes.

It was a pair of tinted goggles.

"Get these on. There's millions of ice crystals in the snow and they're all shining in the sun. They'll make you go blind if you're not careful."

Olly pulled the goggles over his head, and his eyes immediately felt better. He could see clearly as the man chucked him a long-sleeved T-shirt and a fleece and a pair of pants, all his size. The man kept rummaging until he had pulled out a waterproof jacket, and another pair of pants, a hat and a pair of thick gloves.

"First lesson: always have the right gear," the man said. "It keeps you alive."

Olly quickly pulled it all on and straightaway felt a bit warmer.

"Th-thank you," Olly managed to reply.

The man smiled back. A mountain smile that made creases in his tanned face around the corners of his eyes. "Okay. Let's see what we can do about your footwear."

By now Olly's bare feet were numb with cold. The man dug out a pair of thick wool socks, and a pair of lace-up leather boots.

"Try these on for size. If they are a little big that's okay. It will give your feet room to breathe, and the trapped air will keep them warmer than tight-fitting boots."

Olly sat on a rock, nodded blankly back at the man, and pulled the socks on. He immediately felt his feet wrapped up in soft, comfortable warmth. When he pulled the boots on, it was even better. He stood up and took a couple of steps to try them out. They came up above his ankles and gripped on to his legs. He felt he could walk anywhere in them.

"Ankle support and a good grip for slippery surfaces," the man said approvingly. "Just what you need. You'd be amazed how much comes down to a pair of nice, dry feet. And a decent meal, of course. I'll make breakfast. Here." He passed Olly a couple of empty metal canteens. "Fill these up with snow, will you?"

It seemed an odd thing to do, but Olly

did as he was asked. He scooped the snow into the canteens with his gloved hands. While he did that, the man put some oats, honey and water into a pan and started to warm them up over a portable gas stove.

"Now screw the tops on those canteens," the man told him, "and slide them inside your shirt. Your body heat will melt the snow. The air up here is very, very dry, so we're going to need a lot of water as we go. We could stay nice and warm in our clothes but still die of thirst if we're not careful."

Olly looked around at the ground and the mountains, all covered in white.

"But can't we just eat the snow?" he asked. "It's just frozen water."

The man smiled as if he knew Olly had been about to ask that very question.

"Exactly. It's frozen. Your lips and tongue will end up with painful cold sores, which could get infected. There's lots of ways to die up here, and that's a really silly one!" He smiled broadly and kept stirring the oatmeal that now was bubbling nicely.

Olly's stomach was rumbling. The man produced a couple of metal bowls and they tucked in. Olly had missed the barbecue last night and was so hungry he got through his helping in seconds.

Now that he wasn't going to

freeze to death, or starve, it seemed a good time for an obvious question.

"So, where exactly are we?" Olly asked. His voice sounded loud in the cold, clean air. There was no other noise. Just the whistle of the wind in his ears, which were starting to ache with the cold. He pulled his hat down and his hood up to keep them warm.

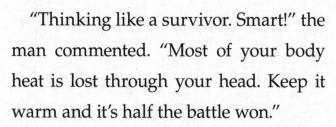

"Thinking like a survivor. Smart!" the man commented. "Most of your body heat is lost through your head. Keep it warm and it's half the battle won."

He pulled on a warm-looking hat of his own.

"As for where we are, we're thirteen thousand feet above sea level."

Olly thought. Thirteen thousand feet was two and a half miles. Straight up.

"That's high," he said nervously.

"It sure is," the man agreed. "It's not for the fainthearted up here. If the cold doesn't kill you, there's a long list of other things that might. A lack of water. Or starvation. Frostbite. Or a bad fall. There's many ways for the unwary to die and only a few ways to stay alive." He held out his hand. "I'm here to help you, buddy – I'll be your guide in these mountains."

Olly shook his hand cautiously.

"I'm Olly. What's your name?"

"My name's Bear. So now we know each other. Okay. Let's get started."

Olly looked around him, bewildered. How was all this happening? Was it related to the compass? And how on earth was he going to get back?

But before he could answer any of these questions Bear spoke again.

"Let's get to it, Olly. Out here, we either get busy living or we get busy dying. There's lots to do. First up, keep topping up the pan with snow; we need as much to drink as we can for the journey ahead."

"What journey ahead?" Olly replied, as he added snow to the pan.

"Our journey to get you back safely."

Together, Bear and Olly boiled the water to make them each a cup of hot, sweet tea. They drank it out of metal cups. The heat warmed Olly's whole body and the sugar pumped energy into his limbs.

"So, Olly." Bear grinned. "Ready for some real adventure?"

"Not really," Olly said honestly. Everything was all so strange, but it didn't change the fact that he just wanted to go home.

"Well, sometimes in life we might not want adventure, but it comes and finds us anyway. Kind of sneaks up on us when we least expect it. That's the magic." Bear paused. "But right now we need to get moving. There's a storm coming and we have to get across these mountains."

"A storm?" Olly said in alarm. He looked up. The sky was totally blue, until he saw where Bear pointed at the horizon. If Olly squinted, he could just see a dark smudge there.

"When that hits," Bear said, "you won't be able to see your hand in front of your face. Drink that tea – we need to get moving."

They packed up the small camp. Bear divided everything between a large backpack for himself and a smaller one for Olly. Bear took the tent, sleeping bag and the cooking equipment. Bear's backpack already had several bundles of clothes tightly packed in watertight clear bags, a lot of black rope, plus a handful of gadgets that Olly didn't recognize.

Olly made a face when he realized he was going to have to carry something.

Bear noticed.

"Only way to do this is as a team, Olly," he said. "We divide the effort and we work hard. Together we will be stronger and that gives us the best chance of staying alive. Got it?"

"But there's so much of it!" Olly said. It reminded him of the pile of stuff he had been told to bring to camp.

Bear smiled. "I know. Tell me about it.

46

But the right equipment can save your life." He paused. "Unless you'd rather freeze to death knowing you could have brought the one thing that would have saved you?"

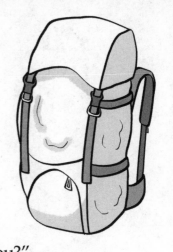

Olly knew he didn't have a choice. This was going to be hard work – a lot harder than building a den. But it was stick with this guy, or be left stranded in the mountains and the storm. He shrugged his backpack on until it was sort of comfortable on his back.

Bear gave the smudge on the horizon a final look.

"It's getting closer," he said grimly. "We should move."

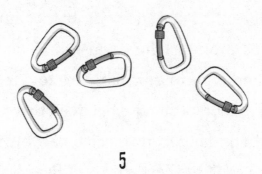

5

WALKING ON WATER

Together, the pair trekked along a deep valley between two giant mountains. Bear told Olly that being on a glacier meant that beneath them wasn't solid ground but solid ice, many hundreds of feet thick.

"When it comes to the wild mountains you have to be prepared or you might not survive." He looked right at Olly. "Out here we are going to fight smart, okay?"

Olly nodded cautiously.

Bear tied one end of his black climbing rope around Olly's waist, and tied the other end to himself, leaving a long stretch of loose rope between them.

"The danger on a glacier is always what you can't see beneath you." Bear tied the final knots. "Together we are stronger. If one of us falls through a hole in the snow into a crevasse beneath, then the other one can stop that fall being fatal." He coiled the rest of the rope around his shoulder, ready for use if needed.

"What's a crevasse?" Olly asked with a sense of dread.

"Crevasses are tears in the ice that get formed as the glacier moves around. They can be hundreds of feet deep. Dark scars carved into the glacier, constantly shifting, often hidden, and one of the

biggest dangers in the high peaks."
He paused. "I was almost killed in a
crevasse many years ago and it taught
me a healthy respect for the mountains.
That's why we rope up. Out here you
will only get it wrong once."

Olly looked down at the knot tied to
him and pulled it extra tight.

* * *

It was hard going when they
set off, and Olly's legs started
to get extra tired, extra quick.
The snow was about four inches
deep, so he had to lift his
foot right out of the snow
with every step before
he could move it
forward and put it
down again.

Even though there was a storm coming, they only made their way slowly along the valley, *plod, plod, plod.* Bear also had a long, carbon fiber pole and he prodded the ground in front of them with every step.

Olly looked back over his shoulder to check the storm's progress, and promptly fell flat on his face as his boots hit a buried rock. His knees stung from scraping against it.

"Careful, champ."

Bear helped Olly up.

"Try to keep looking ahead. We always look

forward – in body and mind. It's also why I use the pole. You never know when there's something beneath the snow. A hole, crevasse or rock could all break your leg. Try to follow where I walk."

"Shouldn't we be hurrying?" Olly asked.

"No. The air's so thin up here that you'd just collapse because your lungs wouldn't be getting enough oxygen. And hurrying makes you sweat, then the sweat turns to ice on your skin, and you get hypothermia. Two more ways to die! So we don't hurry. We'll do better if we just keep going, slow and steady."

"What's hypothermia?" Olly asked as they pressed on.

"Well, your body always tries to keep

itself at the same temperature, about ninety-nine degrees. It's called your core temperature. Hypothermia is when your core drops below that, and your body has to start pulling in blood from your arms and legs to try to keep your brain and core organs warm. It means your hands and feet stop working properly. And if you still don't get warm, and your brain starts to cool down, you then lose the ability to make good decisions, until eventually... well, you get the idea."

Olly thought about that while they walked in silence for a while. Every step was still an effort, though Bear made it look so easy.

He tried to copy the way Bear walked, constantly checking out the ground ahead. He walked with a kind of rhythm. Step and lift foot, step and lift foot, step and lift foot …

Because Olly was concentrating so hard it took him a moment to notice Bear was leading them over to the left-hand side of the valley, instead of heading straight down. He snuck another frustrated look back at the storm. It felt like this guy was determined to make them go slow.

"Why are we going this way?" Olly asked. "Isn't it quicker to go straight?"

"The quickest route isn't always the straightest," Bear told him. He pointed along the top of the right-hand side of the valley. Olly looked up and

saw that, near the top, the sides didn't
slope. They went straight up – and then,
in places, they started to slope outward.

"Can you feel the wind?" he asked
Olly. "It's blowing against the right-hand
side. That means it carves out the snow
on that side of the valley, so it overhangs.

When the overhang gets too heavy, it falls. Then you get a thousand tons of snow dropping on your head from sixteen hundred feet, and, well, then it gets messy."

"Let me guess," Olly said, *"another way to die?"*

"You're getting the hang of it!"

Soon they left the overhang behind them, but the valley was getting narrower. Eventually the steep walls were only about a hundred feet apart, and the ground in between was smooth and flat.

"This is good," Bear told Olly. "We're off the glacier and back on solid ground. The forest will be down ahead of us now."

Bear carefully untied the rope from Olly and coiled it, and then the pair kept moving.

Just when Olly felt they were making good progress down and away from the mountains, Bear suddenly stopped and held up his hand.

"See that?" he asked.

Olly peered ahead and tried to see something different.

"Snow?" he said.

"Yes, but it's completely flat. All the snow we've walked on so far has had bumps in it because of the ground underneath. Whenever I see something different I get suspicious. I want to know what's changed. Wait here."

Bear walked forward slowly, prodding the snow with his pole as he went. Olly stood where he was. He felt the cold seep into his boots and tramped on the spot to warm up his feet. He just wanted to

be moving again.
Bear knelt down
and brushed the
snow away with
his glove. Then he
beckoned to Olly.
"Come and look,
but carefully.
Only step in my
footprints."

Olly walked forward curiously,
carefully putting his feet exactly where
Bear's had been. Where Bear had scraped
away the snow, Olly saw smooth, gray
ice.

"There's a frozen lake under us," Bear
said. He waved a hand at the flat snow
in front of them. "That's why it's so
smooth."

Olly glared at the ground. "Is it safe?" he asked nervously. Suddenly he was afraid to move in case it cracked open beneath him.

"Gray ice like this is usually old and thick," Bear said. "If it was dark, that would mean it was thinner. If it's at least two inches then it's safe." He stood up and rapped on the ice sharply with his pole, three times. "So this should take our weight. Okay. Time to rope up again."

Bear reattached the rope to Olly, this time with a little more distance between them. Then he studied the smooth snow in front of them carefully.

"It's never ideal to have to walk on any ice, but there's no other way around. We'll stick close to the side, where the ice is stronger. We'll go steady – just walk exactly where I walk."

And so they began to make their way carefully along as the rocky mountain faces towered overhead. Every few steps, Bear jammed his pole through the snow to feel the ice underneath. Then he put his foot *exactly* where the pole had been. He took short steps so that Olly could put his feet in Bear's footprints.

Now that Olly knew he was walking on thin ice, he thought he could feel it. It trembled and creaked and groaned, like it might be about to snap. Or was that just his imagination? He couldn't tell. He just knew he would be very glad to get off it.

Up ahead, about sixty feet away, the snowy ground started to go up. That must be the shore of the lake, Olly realized. Once they were there, they would be safe. Olly fixed his eyes on it, watching it get closer, step-by-step. His legs still trembled at the thought of the fragile ice underneath.

Soon the ground was fifteen feet away, on the other side of a few rocks sticking up through the ice. Olly grinned in relief. They were going to make it!

But once again, Bear wasn't heading straight for the shore. He was walking around in a wide curve. The shore was just feet away. How long was he going to keep them out here?

Bear had said stick to the edges, and they were at the edge. Olly decided to make a break for it. He took one, two, three steps. There was a loud *crack*.

"Olly!" Bear shouted in alarm.

Then the ice gave way.

Olly screamed as he plunged into the freezing, dark water.

6

DEADLY UNDERWEAR

It was the coldest thing Olly had ever known. It was agony. The cold was chewing his bones like an animal. It was a million times worse than when you turn the shower to cold by mistake.

He tried to scream again, but the freezing water was like bands of iron around his chest that paralyzed his lungs. It was all Olly could do to draw another breath.

The water was shallow and Olly's head

and shoulders were still above water. Bear grabbed the rope between them and pulled hard on the slack until it went taut. He then rapidly dropped onto the ice and wrapped the rope around his body.

"Use the rope to pull against, Olly," Bear shouted. "Wriggle like a seal and get yourself out, back onto the ice. Work quickly, Olly, come on!"

But Olly couldn't do it. He was floundering around in shock and numbed by the cold. He could hardly even keep himself from slipping beneath the water.

Bear saw that Olly was struggling and reacted fast. He flung himself flat, rope in one hand, holding Olly in tight against the edge of the hole and the other arm outstretched toward him.

"Grab my hand!"

Olly reached out, but he was shivering so hard that he had to force his hand to go toward Bear's. Shock, cold and fear were stopping him.

Bear's strong fingers closed around his wrist and he pulled Olly up and out of the hole. Then he started dragging him away from the danger and toward solid ground. Bear then quickly started unlacing Olly's boots.

"You need to get this wet gear off!" Bear ordered.

"But I'll die!" Olly howled.

"You'll die if you don't," he replied. "Wet clothes will steal the heat away from your body fifty times faster than dry clothes. You need to get them off. Now move it!"

Olly started to peel off his boots and

clothes, all the way down to his shorts. He noticed that his hands weren't working so well and were shaking frantically with the cold. The material clung to his body like  wet plaster, and the freezing air on his skin gave him goose bumps. Bear rapidly pulled a man-sized shirt out of his backpack and threw it to Olly, along with dry shorts.

"Put these on. Wet underwear could kill you. And this hat and dry socks."

Bear took off his waterproof coat and placed it down on the ground. "Stand on this and start marching fast on the spot. Good.

Now, keep going!"

Bear started to wring streams of water out of Olly's clothes.

"W-w-what's the point of this marching?" Olly complained. "I'm tired."

"Your body is in shock and you've

had a huge dose of adrenaline and fear to deal with." He paused. "Marching up and down will help keep you warm."

So Olly kept marching.

Bear fished the gas stove out and packed more snow into the metal saucepan. While they waited for the snow to melt, Bear stuffed another pair of socks into Olly's boots to soak up as much water as they could. And he asked the question Olly had been dreading.

"So, what happened back there?"

"I didn't follow you," Olly admitted.

Bear looked at him. "I was near the edge, and I thought it would be easy to reach it. I'm sorry."

"Did you see the rocks sticking up through the ice? They break up the ice and make it thin. Even near the edge of the lake." Bear paused. "Olly, we're a team, and we will survive together. We all make mistakes sometimes. It's okay. Just do your best to keep focused." Bear paused again, then said seriously, "You were on borrowed time there. The combination of cold, shock and fear numbs the body's senses and makes it almost impossible to do even simple tasks. That's how people drown so fast in cold water. Next time you might not be so lucky!"

He rolled Olly's clothes in the powdery snow to absorb more of the moisture, then beat the snow off them again. Olly's legs were aching more than ever. More than anything he just wanted to stop and lie down. His feet stumbled.

"I don't think I can go on much longer," he complained.

Bear was spreading Olly's clothes out flat on a rock. He didn't look up.

"A hundred years ago," he said, "a man called Ernest Shackleton led an expedition to the South Pole. One of his men fell off the ice into the sea. They fished him out, but they didn't have anything to make a fire with. So he just had to walk in circles until he was dried out. It took him twelve hours. Twelve hours of freezing cold and pain."

"Twelve hours!" Olly gasped.

"Yes. Grim, eh? But guess what? He lived. That's our goal too. Fortunately we can make a fire, so we can get a hot drink inside you."

Olly started to slow down.

"Keep going, Olly. That's your part of the deal. And remember, if it was easy, anyone could do it."

Olly pictured that poor man at the South Pole. Twelve hours, and nothing to warm him up at the end of it.

"Besides," Bear added, "I don't think we've got twelve hours." He shot a dirty look at the sky and Olly remembered the storm. He looked back the way they had come, but he couldn't see the smudge. He was about to say so, when he realized why he couldn't see it.

It wasn't a smudge anymore. It had grown. When they had started to walk, Olly had been able to see the mountains miles away in the distance. Now the smudge had gotten much closer and it was big enough to hide the mountains completely.

The snow melted and boiled. Bear

made a cup of hot tea which Olly drank as he marched. His shivers made the rim of the mug clatter against his teeth, but he felt the heat of the tea warming him from the inside out.

"Okay, I think we're there," said Bear at last. Olly's clothes had now frozen stiff in the freezing air. Bear bashed them against the ground so that bits of ice flew in all directions. He tossed Olly's pants over to him.

"Here. Try those."

Olly put them on again and, amazingly, they were almost completely dry.

But Olly winced when he pulled on

his boots. Despite everything Bear had done, and another fresh pair of socks, they were still cold and damp inside.

"Damp is better than wet," Bear said directly. "Meanwhile you can stuff your wet socks down your pants to dry them out. Okay, now we need to press on." He gave the sky another look. "We might *just* be able to get out of this valley before the storm hits." He pointed. "See that bend ahead? If the valley ends after that, then maybe we can drop down to lower ground and find some shelter."

So together the pair started to move again.

Olly trudged on after Bear. For the time being his feet were dry in thick, new socks, but he could feel the cold of his wet boots soaking through. Eventually he would have to change them, but for now he knew he just had to deal with it. After all, if he had listened to Bear, he wouldn't have fallen into the water in the first place.

Plus the thought of finding shelter from the storm gave him new strength.

It got darker as they walked. Back when they had started, the snow had shone so bright in the sun that Olly couldn't see without the snow goggles. Now he had to pull the goggles down around his neck just to see clearly.

They reached the bend in the valley. Olly's hopes were at their highest as they came around the corner.

Then they came tumbling down.

The rocky sides just kept going. It wasn't the end of the valley. There was still no way out except to go forward.

Olly was so tired, and he couldn't see anywhere they could shelter. He looked back at the approaching storm. It filled the valley behind them. He couldn't see where they had been. It was all just a mass of swirling snow.

"We're too late," Bear said grimly. "It's going to hit us."

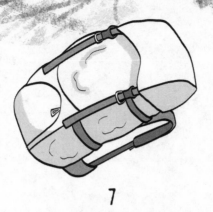

7

DIGGING IN

Olly felt his heart sink as he gazed at the storm. Clouds as high as the mountains were charging down toward them. He didn't feel he had any more strength in his body. His legs didn't want to take another step.

But he would have to. He would force himself to keep up.

To Olly's surprise, Bear didn't keep on going. Instead he went to the side of the valley, where the ground started to slope

and the snow was much deeper. He dropped his backpack on the ground, thrust both gloved hands into the snow and scooped out a handful.

"Give me a hand?" he asked as he threw it to one side.

Olly blinked. What was Bear doing? How would digging a hole in the snow help?

Olly didn't understand, but Bear was asking for his help and that was enough for him. He hurried to Bear's side and they started to dig out a hole together. Olly copied the way Bear did it and put his hands together like a shovel to scoop out chunks of snow the size of soccer balls.

"I reckon the snow here's about twelve feet deep," Bear said as they dug. "It's perfect for what we want. Frozen solid on top, powdery underneath."

"Why are we making a hole?" Olly asked.

"It's going to be more than just a hole. We're going to spend the night here."

"What?" Olly stopped digging and stared at him. "In the snow?"

"Best place." Bear didn't stop. After a moment, Olly went back to digging as well. He had thought the tent back at camp was uncomfortable. But spending a night under snow?

"We'll freeze to death!" he argued as he dug. "Snow's so cold."

"It is," Bear agreed, "but it's also one of the best insulators in nature. Snow has millions of air bubbles trapped in it, which hold the warmth amazingly. This shelter will keep the cold air out and trap our warmth in. Clever, huh?"

Olly nodded. "Kind of like the Inuit in the Arctic when they use snow to make igloos?"

"Exactly." Bear smiled. "Although we'll be *under* the snow, not on top of it."

Olly's arms ached. He couldn't dig any longer.

"I don't think I can go on," Olly said. "It hurts so much."

Bear stopped digging. "I never promised that this journey would be easy," he calmly replied, "but if you can find the strength inside you, you can overcome all things. Keep going, buddy."

Olly kept digging.

The pair quietly worked together as a team. Bear didn't need to tell Olly what to do. It just sort of happened.

The longer the
tunnel got, the
harder it was to
throw the loose
snow out at the end.
So Olly would scoop it up behind him
into lumps and throw it out into the open.

Olly found he had a strange feeling. It
was a feeling he wasn't used to.

He was enjoying this.

He wasn't sure whether it was the
teamwork he liked, or maybe the danger.
Perhaps it was simply the fact that he was
doing something that would help keep
him alive. Whatever it was, he liked it.

Olly kept going.

He knew they were still in danger,
but he believed that together they could
handle it. His feet were still cold, but he

would soon change his socks. At first his arms ached more and more as they dug, but then suddenly they felt fine. Tired, but fine. His body had gotten used to it.

And for the first time in his life, Olly felt proud of what he was making. Really proud. He smiled to himself.

Bear crawled back out of the tunnel when it was nearly seven feet long.

"Now we need a wall across the entrance," he said. "Like this."

There were piles of freshly dug snow all around the entrance to the tunnel. Bear used his hands to work some of it into a block. Olly found that making blocks was like making square snowballs. He could press the white powder into small lumps, and then press them together to make bigger lumps. Bear showed him how to lay the first blocks in a line on the ground about one and a half feet from the hole. Then he put more blocks down on top of them.

"What's this for?" Olly asked as he worked.

"The tunnel faces into the wind. We need the wall to keep the wind out. It's the wind that will kill you fastest up in these mountains."

Olly carried on making blocks while Bear crawled back into the tunnel.

"Good work, Olly," he shouted back. "We're really getting there now. But there's still a bit more to do."

"More?" Olly asked.

"Well, we've dug *in*. Now we need to dig *up*."

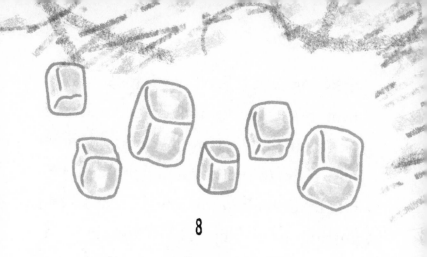

8

SNUG

Bear started to dig so that the tunnel sloped upward. Outside, the first snowflakes began to fall.

When Olly looked up from building his wall, he could see millions of them whirling around in the middle of the approaching storm.

It was only a matter of time until they would be engulfed in the blizzard.

Olly made the wall higher as the flakes whipped around him in the growing wind. Each block took a bit of time, but he made himself keep working and doing the job well. He knew now why everything they had done that day had taken a bit more time than he liked. Testing each step, not walking in a straight line, choosing the harder place to dig.

It had been so they could do it properly. And do it only once.

Now that he knew what the wall was for, Olly realized he couldn't afford to go so fast that the blocks weren't any good or the wall would fall down.

He was learning that in the wild you don't always get second chances.

When it was the same height as Olly, Bear told him it was big enough. Olly happily crawled back into the tunnel.

As soon as he was back in, he was surprised by how warm he felt. Well, warm*er*. It was because his wall blocked out the wind. But when he breathed out a puff of air, he could see it whirling in front of him.

"It's still pretty cold," he pointed out.

"Sure," Bear agreed with a laugh. He had dug the tunnel upward for about a foot or two, then started to dig sideways. "It's still freezing! If it wasn't then all this snow would melt and the cave would collapse. But it won't get any colder. Outside, we'd freeze to death in that wind. In here it's a steady temperature, around thirty-two degrees, and our clothes can keep us warm."

Olly kept on clearing out the fresh piles of snow behind him. Every time he stuck his head outside, the snowflakes had grown thicker. The wind was starting to howl like some kind of animal. He couldn't see more than a couple of feet in any direction. Everything was just white. Even though he had his hood up, the cold turned his face numb.

It was a relief to pull his head back into the tunnel.

Eventually they had carved out a small snow cave at the end of the tunnel. It was big enough to lie down in, but not stand up. Even Olly only had room to kneel.

"We're higher than the end of the tunnel," Olly observed, as they brushed the floor smooth.

"Exactly. Cold air sinks, and warm air rises, so the cold air will go down the tunnel while the air up here stays warm. Now help me smooth down the ceiling, so it doesn't start to drip on us when the snow warms up with our body heat."

Together they brushed at the ceiling with their gloved hands until it was as smooth as it could be.

By the end, they were both covered in loose white powder.

"And the very last job," Bear said, "is to brush yourself off. Snow on your clothes will melt and make them damp."

"Which makes you cold," Olly said with a smile.

Bear grinned at him. "You're learning."

They took turns to knock the loose snow off their clothes at the entrance to the tunnel. By now there was a full storm raging outside. Back in their little snow cave, the air barely moved.

It was very dim because the only light came from the tunnel entrance. Bear used his backpack to block it off, and then there was no light at all, so he flicked on a flashlight. He pulled a

tarpaulin from his pack and laid it down on the floor.

"We sit and lie on this, for insulation," he explained. "Otherwise the snow will suck the heat right out of our bodies." He pulled a couple of energy bars out of his backpack. "This is dinner. Have you got the water?"

Olly had refilled the canteens full of snow several times during the day. The freezing mountain air was bone-dry and they had to drink a lot. Now he pulled them out of his coat for the last time that day.

They tucked into their bars and washed them down with melted snow water. Olly was just knocking back the last drops when he had a thought. What goes in comes out – eventually.

"Uh, so …" he began. "What do I do if I need to, uh … go?"

"Down there." Bear pointed at the bottom of the slope in the tunnel. "Let it soak into the snow, then cover it up with loose powder. We can't go outside now until the storm has passed. But it will pass. Storms always do."

Olly looked where Bear was pointing and grimaced.

After that, the only thing to do was wait out the storm. It was howling outside, but in here it sounded like it was a long way off. Olly lay down and pulled the padded hood of his coat up to act like a pillow.

He had never felt happier in his life. Which was strange considering the danger and discomfort he was in.

He looked around at what they had made together.

"You know, this is actually pretty cool," he said drowsily.

Bear smiled.

"A strong team, good preparation and a bit of effort, and you can manage almost anything."

As Bear talked, Olly could feel sleep creeping up on him. He was bone tired. He had been walking all day, and then he hadn't stopped for even a moment in the rush to dig the shelter out. He blushed to think how he had lied to duck out of building the den with Jack and Omar. He had thought

that was too much effort! It seemed
such a long time ago.

Then his heavy eyes closed – asleep.

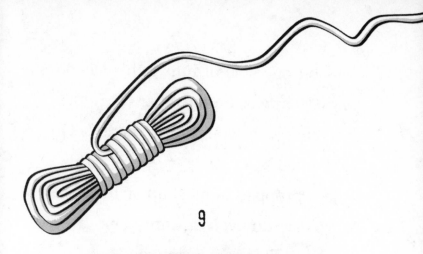

9

TWO HANDS, TWO FEET

Olly woke up after the best night's sleep he had ever had. He snuggled into his pillow and wondered what time it was. A stab of hunger answered his question.

Breakfast time! He was looking forward to some more of that oatmeal before the adventure ahead.

He opened his eyes ... and found himself looking at Jack.

Olly sat bolt upright in surprise. He looked around him in confusion. Jack was on one side of him in his sleeping bag. Omar was on the other.

"What are you doing here?" Olly exclaimed.

Jack propped himself up on his elbow.

"What do you mean?" he asked sleepily. "This is our tent, too."

Olly looked around wide-eyed. Where was the snow cave?

He felt something hard on the ground next to him. It was the compass. Olly stared at it.

What had happened? How had he gotten back here?

Then Omar groaned as he sat up.

"Man, that ground is so hard. I don't reckon I can do another night like that."

Olly remembered what Bear had told him.

"If you can find the strength inside you, you can overcome all things," he said under his breath. "All you need is to keep going."

Omar stared at him. "What are you on about?" He paused. "Keep going! That's funny coming from the guy who gave up altogether and left his friends to do all the hard work yesterday."

"Yesterday?" Olly said in surprise.

If the den building had been yesterday … that meant everything with

Bear had happened all in one night. Without the other two noticing.

Had it just been a really vivid dream?

"Don't tell me you don't remember," Omar sneered.

"No," Olly said quietly. "I remember."

Jack tried to break up the tension. He clambered out of his bag.

"We should get moving," he said. "What's up today, after breakfast?"

Omar was still glaring at Olly. A good night's sleep clearly hadn't done anything to change Omar's opinion of him.

"You think I'll let you down again, don't you?" Olly said quietly.

Omar just shrugged.

"Whatever."

"I won't. I promise," Olly told him.

He got the idea nothing he said would convince Omar he had changed. Olly knew that he would just have to show him. "Maybe I'll surprise you," Olly said with a smile, then started to climb out of the tent.

* * *

Olly looked up at the climbing wall and tried not to feel nervous.

He wanted to do this. He really did. It wasn't just that he wanted to show Omar and Jack. It was because they were meant to do this as a team, and Omar and Jack were his team.

And he wanted to do this for himself. To feel that sense of pride again.

But it was a long way up and he had never really climbed before.

The wall was forty feet high, and

shaped like a real rock face. There were ropes dangling down which attached to metal clips on the front of their harnesses, so if anyone slipped then they wouldn't fall and hurt themselves. Everyone watched as an instructor demonstrated how to climb. She was already halfway up.

"You've got two hands and two feet," she called down at them. "So always make sure that three out of four are holding on to something.

Only ever move one at a time, like me …"

She made it look so easy. In fact, she reminded Olly a little of Bear. She could make it look easy because she was very good at it, and she had put in a lot of hard work to get there.

"You are going to climb up three at a time, against the clock and we'll see which team is the fastest. First group up for the Yellow team is … Jack, Olly and Omar!"

A lot of kids looked quite happy that someone else was going first. They could make the mistakes for everyone else to learn from.

The instructors came forward with helmets and harnesses. Jack started to put his on without any help because he had done this before. Olly got tangled up, and an instructor had to help him out. And by the time they were both done, Omar was helmeted, harnessed and ready to go.

Eventually the three boys took their places at the foot of the wall. Olly was in the middle, with Omar on his left and Jack on his right.

"You going to drop out, Olly?" Omar whispered. "Just tell them you don't like

heights and they'll let me and Jack do it on our own."

Olly just shook his head. He knew Omar would never believe he could do this, until he saw it.

"Get ready!" an instructor called. The boys braced themselves. The instructor was poised with a stopwatch.

"Get set ... Go!"

Olly swallowed his nerves, grabbed hold of the wall, and started to climb.

10

TEAMWORK!

It wasn't long before Olly felt fire in every joint of his body. His shoulders and hips felt like someone was slowly pulling his arms and legs off.

It wasn't like the way his arms had ached as he scooped out the snow with Bear, or how his legs had felt like lead weights after trekking through the mountains. Every movement he made on the wall had to haul the weight of his body upward, which meant that everything he did was against gravity. Climbing used different muscles than walking, and his muscles were making sure he knew about it.

But Olly kept going.

He still had the advice from the instructors ringing in his ears, about how you should only move one part of your body at a time. So that was what he did. It was like when he had walked with Bear. There was a rhythm to it. Move foot. Lift body. Move hand. Lift body.

And above all, just keep going.

And Olly used another trick he had picked up from his adventure in the mountains. Bear had been looking ahead every step of the way. He always knew exactly where he was going to put each foot before he put it down. So Olly tried the same trick with the rock face. By looking up, he could always see where the next handholds and footholds were, so he was ready and could move fast.

Olly used to just give up the moment he started feeling tired or uncomfortable. But something had changed in him. It was as if the storm had made him stronger. He knew now that some things take effort. The feeling of being part of a team gave him new strength. Sure, it was tiring, but it wasn't anything he couldn't handle.

The three boys were practically neck and neck as they climbed together. But then Omar grabbed for a handhold too quickly and suddenly his fingers slipped off the wall. He fell two feet backward with an angry shout.

His rope caught him and he dangled
awkwardly in midair.

Omar managed to get one foot and
one hand on the wall, but his body still
wobbled and he couldn't find anywhere
else to grab.

Olly instinctively stopped climbing.
His teammate needed him.

"To your right!" Olly called. He had spotted the handhold a moment earlier.

Omar grabbed at the wall on his right. "A bit lower …"

Omar moved his hand, and he was able to grab a bump of rock and hold himself steady.

His eyes met Olly's. "Got it," he said.

Jack had also stopped climbing to watch what was happening, so none of them had gotten too far ahead. Then all three boys started climbing again. Steady, together, with renewed purpose and effort.

And in no time, the trio reached the top of the wall – together.

The leaders helped them over the edge at the top while the kids on the ground were cheering. They had done it! Olly saw Jack and Omar's happy grins, and then he realized he was grinning too.

Then Omar held up a fist with his knuckles toward him.

"Good job, team," he said. "And thanks for the help."

Olly and Omar bumped fists together.

After the climbing, they had an hour to themselves and they headed back to their tent. On their way they passed the soccer field, where a five-a-side match between the Yellow and Red teams had just finished. As the boys walked past, a girl close to them suddenly screamed and Olly recognized her as the girl who didn't like creepy-crawlies.

Back at the tent they had a small victory feast to celebrate the climb. Olly had some granola bars, and Omar produced some crackers, and Jack had a bottle of juice. Together they sat and shared the treats.

Then Jack suddenly stopped and wriggled, as if he was sitting on something uncomfortable. He reached under Olly's sleeping bag.

He held up the object and examined it.

"Hey, Olly, what did you bring these for?"

Olly looked up and saw what Jack was holding.

Olly felt his heart start to pound.

A pair of goggles.

But not just any old pair of goggles. These were the very same goggles which Bear had given him in the mountains.

Olly felt his heart pound.

If the snow goggles were real, then so was the rest of it! Maybe the compass would show him its fifth direction again so he could get back there.

How could he get the compass to do it again?

But then he thought of what Bear might say. If you were part of a team then you didn't just do things for yourself. And Olly knew someone who needed the compass more than him.

So Olly put his drink down.

"Back in a minute, guys!" he said as he crawled out of the tent.

He didn't know where to look, but he didn't need to. He heard a familiar scream from a tent nearby. The flap pulled back and a girl crawled out. She was muttering to herself something about nasty insects and she sounded really angry.

She looked up and saw him. "What do you want?" she snapped.

Olly could see that she was embarrassed. She'd turned bright red.

"I just want to give you this," he said. He held out the compass. "It's a gift."

"What is it?" she asked.

"Your adventure," Olly replied, and smiled.

The End

Bear Grylls got the taste for adventure at a young age from his father, a former Royal Marine. After school, Bear joined the Reserve SAS, then went on to become one of the youngest people to ever climb Mount Everest, just two years after breaking his back in three places during a parachute jump.

Among other adventures he has led expeditions to the Arctic and the Antarctic, crossed oceans and set world records in skydiving and paragliding.

Bear is also a bestselling author and the host of television programs such as *Survival School* and *The Island*.

He has shared his survival skills with people all over the world, and has taken many famous movie stars and sports stars on adventures – and even President Barack Obama!

Bear Grylls is Chief Scout to the UK Scouting Association, encouraging young people to have great adventures, follow their dreams and to look after their friends.

When Bear's not traveling the world, he lives with his wife and three sons on a barge in London, or on an island off the coast of Wales.

Find out more at **www.beargrylls.com**

Experience all the adventures ...

AVAILABLE NOW